To Angela

First US edition 2020

Library of Congress Catalog Card Number pending
ISBN 978-1-5362-1530-4

20 21 22 23 24 25 CCP 10 9 8 7 6 5 4 3 2 1

Printed in Shenzhen, Guangdong, China

This book was typeset in Neutraface Display.
The illustrations were done in pencil and watercolor.

Candlewick Press
99 Dover Street
Somerville, Massachusetts 02144

www.candlewick.com

If Winter Comes, Tell It I'm Not Here

SIMONA CIRAOLO

CANDLEWICK PRESS

Swimming
is my favorite thing.

I am very good at it.
I really could have
been a fish.

Not many things can drag me out of the water.

"You'd better make the most of it while it lasts.
Summer's going to end soon," says my sister.
"What happens when the summer ends?" I ask.

"Well, first comes fall. The days get shorter,
there's a chill in the air, and the trees lose all their leaves.

You won't need your swimsuit anymore,

so you can kiss *that* goodbye.

Then winter comes. It will be dark all the time.
The cold rain will soon turn to snow. You'll be stuck on the sofa for day

Everything will be SO dull, and you'll be SO cold,
you wouldn't even *dream* of eating ice cream."

I don't want to believe her,
but Mom and Dad say it's true.

There's nothing I can do, except wait.

So I look out for the signs of winter.

One by one, they come, just as my sister said they would.

There's a chill in the air.
The trees begin to lose
their leaves.

Days get shorter and nights come early.
We are all stuck on the sofa.

It rains a lot.

You couldn't stay dry even if you tried.

I haven't wanted to eat any ice cream—not once.

In the end, winter is nothing like I imagined.

I think I like it. I can still have lots of fun!

And even when all the color has
been taken out of the world,
I would never call it dull.

So I figure I better make
the most of it.

Just in case it doesn't
last very long.